A Dog Like Sam

A Dog Like Sam

Edward van de Vendel

Illustrated by
Philip Hopman

Translated by
David Colmer

Eerdmans Books for Young Readers
Grand Rapids, Michigan

Eerdmans Books for Young Readers,
an imprint of
Wm. B. Eerdmans Publishing Co.
2140 Oak Industrial Drive N.E., Grand Rapids, Michigan 49505
www.eerdmans.com/youngreaders

Originally published as *Toen kwam Sam* by
Em. Querido's Kinderboeken Uitgeverij
Text © 2011 Edward van de Vendel
Illustrations © 2011 Philip Hopman

Printed in the United States of America

22 21 20 19 18 17 16   1 2 3 4 5 6 7

Library of Congress Cataloging-in-Publication Data

Names: Vendel, Edward van de, author. | Hopman, Philip, illustrator. |
  Colmer, David, 1960- translator.
Title: A dog like Sam / by Edward van de Vendel ; illustrated by Philip
  Hopman ; translated by David Colmer.
Other titles: Toen kwam Sam. English
Description: Grand Rapids, MI : Eerdmans Books for Young Readers, 2016. |
  Summary: Kix and Emilia adopt a stray dog and name him Sam, even though
  their parents say they cannot keep him, but then Sam's original owner
  comes looking for him.
Identifiers: LCCN 2015050587 | ISBN 9780802854841 (hardback)
Subjects: | CYAC: Dogs—Fiction. | Family life—Fiction. | BISAC: JUVENILE
  FICTION / Animals / Dogs. | JUVENILE FICTION / Family / General (see also
  headings under Social Issues). | JUVENILE FICTION / Animals / Pets.
Classification: LCC PZ7.V556 Doc 2016 | DDC [Fic]—dc23
LC record available at https://lccn.loc.gov/2015050587

Nederlands
N letterenfonds   The publisher gratefully acknowledges the support
dutch foundation   of the Dutch Foundation for Literature.
for literature

MIX
Paper from
responsible sources
FSC® C005010
www.fsc.org

A Dog Like Sam

1

The dog came out of nowhere.

It was standing at the end of the driveway with its front paws on the gravel and its back paws on the road.

Kix was lying on the grass. It was summer, and he was reading a funny book about a pig going to the movies. Next to him, on the blue blanket, his little sister Emilia was doing a puzzle.

Kix heard snuffling. Very quiet snuffling.

"Hey," he said. "Look. There."

"I'm busy," Emilia said.

"No, really," Kix said, and then Emilia looked up and she saw it too — a white dog.

The dog was big and soft and looked like it was too scared to come any closer. As if it was wondering whether it had stopped at the right address. It turned its head to the left, toward the horses, and sniffed. The horses didn't look up, they were too busy munching their hay — they'd just got a fresh batch — and then the dog sniffed to the right, in the direction of Kix and Emilia.

"Hello, dog," Emilia said. "Come closer, onto the lawn. It's okay. I'm Emilia, and this is Kix."

"It doesn't understand that," Kix said.

"Yes, it does," Emilia said. "This is a smart dog."

Maybe his sister was right. The dog didn't look the least

bit stupid. But there was something strange about it, something Kix couldn't quite figure out. It didn't come any closer — it just stood there with its nose up, testing the air.

Kix stood up and took a few steps toward the gravel. It seemed to startle the dog, who half-turned away from him. Now it could run off at any moment, back onto the road.

"Kix," Emilia said, "you have to be careful. I want a white dog. I want this one. I want to keep it."

Kix turned back to his sister. "Shh, not so loud!"

But maybe he did that a little too loudly himself, because when he turned around again, the white dog was gone. It had disappeared.

2

"It was like a ghost dog," Kix said.

They were in the car with their mother. Emilia had swimming lessons, but they were early, so they were going to the grocery store first.

"A phantom," Kix said. No answer came. Emilia was daydreaming and gazing out the window. Mom turned into the parking lot.

A little later they were walking down the aisles. Kix was pushing the cart, and Mom was rushing around grabbing everything they needed. Emilia wanted to go in the child seat, but Kix wouldn't let her, because then he'd have to go extra slow. They argued about it, but not for long. When they reached the checkout, Emilia said, "It wasn't a phantom. It was real."

"You don't know that," Kix said. "You can't be sure. Maybe it came from a ghost world with ghost animals. Maybe it doesn't exist at all and we were seeing something that doesn't exist. And the ghost world is white, just like the dog. The moon's white, and so are the trees and the buildings, and there aren't any sounds. You only hear panting. Or screams. Yeah, you hear screams, but only at night, and in the ghost world with the ghost animals it's always night, and the bats are white too — "

"Mommy!" Emilia cried. "Kix is being mean. He's scaring me!"

Of course, Kix didn't believe it himself — all that stuff about a ghost world. And at the swimming pool he was already thinking about something completely different. While they were waiting for Emilia to finish her lesson, Mom let Kix get a toy from the vending machine. It was a little plastic crane you had to put together yourself. Childish, really, even if it did take him ages.

But when they got home, there it was again, on the lawn near the road — the big white dog.

6

3

This time the dog came closer. It wasn't an apparition from a ghost world after all. It was real and true. Mom, Kix, and Emilia stood next to the car, waiting to see what it would do.

It took a couple of steps on the grass near the road. And then a couple more onto the first few feet of their gravel driveway.

"Doggy!" Emilia called.

The big white dog stopped where it was. It looked at them and wagged its tail slowly from side to side.

"What a magnificent animal," Mom sighed.

Kix looked at her. Mom loved dogs, he knew that, but he'd always thought she liked little dogs better than big ones. Holly was hers. Holly was old and sweet-tempered. She fit on your lap perfectly and loved being petted. She'd been Mom's dog for a very long time. That was why Dad had wanted a dog last year too, one for himself. Mom, Kix, and Emilia gave him an energetic medium-sized puppy for his birthday. She was called Springer, and she was always happy. Whenever Springer saw Dad, she'd jump up against him and scamper up his legs into his arms.

Kix loved both Holly and Springer. But they were Mom's dog and Dad's dog. Emilia and Kix didn't have a dog of their own. Not one. And now a big, beautiful white dog was standing there staring at them for the second time.

Where did it come from?

Who did it belong to?

Kix walked a few steps down the driveway toward the dog. Emilia followed him. Mom stayed where she was, next to the car.

The white dog watched their every move. It didn't take its eyes off them, but at the same time it seemed to be trying to push its front paws deeper into the gravel.

Kix stood still. So did Emilia.

"Milly," Kix whispered, "I want to keep it too."

"Yes," Emilia whispered.

And then Kix sank to his knees. He didn't know why, he just did it.

"I want to keep you," Kix whispered to the big white dog. "I want to keep you."

And then it happened.

The dog started walking.

Toward Kix.

It walked toward him as if it had just decided that it was okay. That it was agreeing that from now on it would be Kix and Emilia's dog.

4

The big white dog had almost reached Kix.

But it was walking slowly now, very slowly. One step. Another. One more step.

It was still wagging its tail, but more and more cautiously. The tail was drooping lower and lower too. The dog kept its head down, with only its eyes looking up. There were a few long hairs hanging down in front of its eyes.

"Come on," Emilia said. And Kix said, "Nice dog, good dog."

They held out their hands.

Only then did the dog take the last step forward. Now it was only a few feet away. When they stretched out toward it, their fingertips just reached its head.

It felt soft.

Very soft.

They slid forward, closer to its hair and ears and nose. The dog watched their every move, but stayed where it was. It let Kix pet it, and then Emilia too.

They saw the bands of dark hair that ran up its nose to its forehead. They felt the beautiful white hair that hung down over the rest of its strong body. Its hair was matted — you could see that — and its feet were muddy too.

But the dog still shone. Its coat was so white it almost hurt your eyes. It was like snow, but dry and warm. Kix suddenly wanted to press his face into it.

He didn't, though. This dog liked things calm, so Kix stayed calm.

"It's not a ghost dog," Kix whispered after a while. "I was just kidding. But it is a fairy-tale dog."

Emilia just nodded.

She felt the thick folds of skin and hair under the dog's mouth. Emilia could bury her whole hand in them, and the dog didn't mind.

But then it started and jumped backward.

Kix and Emilia were left with their hands in mid-air. They looked around. Mom had taken a step closer.

"No, boy, it's okay," Mom said. "There's no need to be scared. Here, boy, come back."

But the dog was already leaving. It wandered out of their yard and back onto the road.

Kix, Emilia, and their mother watched to see where it would go. It crossed the road. And Mom said, "Oh, now I get it. He belongs to Mr. and Mrs. Jones."

Now it was Kix's turn to be startled, because that was not good news. It was very bad news. Kix didn't like Mr. and Mrs. Jones. They lived on the farm across the road, and they were old and mean. They used to have a snake in a big glass terrarium. One time Dad made Kix go over there with him to say hello to the Joneses. They stood in front of that creepy glass box. There were dead mice in it, and the snake was slowly slithering out of the knot it had tied itself up in. "You'd better watch out," Mr. Jones said. "If that yappy little mutt of yours comes into my yard, Rotter here will swallow him in one bite."

Rotter was the snake. Kix thought it was a stupid joke, and so did Dad.

"You watch out," Dad said. "If that snake of yours comes anywhere near my property, you'll get it back in two pieces."

Mr. Jones didn't think *that* was a very nice joke either, and the visit was soon over.

Kix hadn't been back since — even though the Joneses sold Rotter the snake ages ago. That's what Mrs. Jones told Mom. "It tried to eat the cat," she said, and Kix didn't even know if she was making it up.

How could the white dog be theirs?

Following Mom and Emilia into the house, Kix suddenly imagined something terrible: their fairy-tale dog locked up in the big glass snake box. With a lid on it.

5

They were eating mashed potatoes. Kix liked mashed potatoes, and when he liked his food, he didn't hear what was being said at the table. Eating and listening at the same time was too difficult for him. Besides, his father mostly just talked about the buildings he was building, and Kix already knew all about them. Sometimes he went to Dad's work with him. His mother talked about the music lessons she gave at school, and he definitely didn't need to hear that: he was in her class.

But that was before. Now Kix wasn't even paying attention to his mashed potatoes. It was because of the white dog. He knew it was stupid, but he kept imagining the dog in that glass box. Kix fidgeted with his food and moved his spoon twice as slowly as normal. That was why he only heard the last part of what Mom was saying: ". . . really a superb creature!"

Kix looked up, and so did Emilia. Mom was talking about the dog! What else had she said? Dad started laughing. "No, no, no!" he cried. "We're not getting another dog! We've already got Holly, we've got Springer, and this last year we got those two extra horses on loan too. No, no, no!"

"Honey," Mom said, "I'm not saying — "

She didn't get to finish her sentence, because Emilia mumbled something. She had a very quiet voice, and she was talking to her plate more than to Mom and Dad, but they knew what Emilia was like. Sometimes Emilia brooded over a sentence like it was an egg. A very expensive egg. And then you had better pay attention.

"Umm . . ." she said to her peas and mashed potatoes, "what's the biggest number there is?"

Dad answered. "A trillion, I think. Or a zillion. Why do you ask?"

Emilia held up a finger. "Dad . . . this dog is different from all the other zillion dogs in the world."

Kix nodded. He usually thought his sister was kind of annoying, but not now.

"Oh," Dad said, sighing slightly.

Mom sighed too, but smiled while she was at it.

Kix didn't do anything. He waited, because he knew Emilia wasn't finished.

And he was right.

She said, "This dog has been through different things than all the other zillion dogs in the world. We want to keep him. And we know what his name is. Do you know what his name is, Dad? His name is Sam."

6

That evening Kix crept into his sister's bedroom. "We'll talk about it tomorrow," was what Dad had said at the dinner table, but Kix wanted to talk about it now, right this minute.

Kix sat down on the floor, next to Emilia's bed. There were big cushions there, so he could duck down behind them if Mom came in. "Is the dog really called Sam?" he asked.

"Yep," Emilia said. "That's what his name is."

"Okay," said Kix. Because it was a good name. Sam was a real Sam.

"What you said was right too," Kix whispered. "About Sam being different from other dogs. And you know what?"

"What?" said Emilia, sitting up straight in bed.

"He's a sad dog. Did you see his eyes?"

"Yes," Emilia said, "they're sad eyes."

"That's why we have to keep him, Milly. And look after him. We'd be good at that."

"Yes," said Emilia.

Kix looked at her, and she looked back. They had made a decision. And they knew it was a good decision because of a bark. And another bark.

The barks were coming from outside. From Sam.

7

The next morning Kix and Emilia discovered where Sam had spent the night.

Not that long ago Mom and Dad had built a beautiful new stable close to the field. Next to it was the old horse shed. It used to have a door, but that had been gone for years. And that meant you could look straight in and see what was inside: Dad's first BMW, which had lost its engine, the lawn mower, the ping-pong table, and their old couch too. The couch was covered with dust and straw, left over from the horses, and when Kix looked closely, he saw a few tufts of white hair.

"See?" he said. "Sam slept here. Because he wants to stay with us. Come on!"

He crept into the shed with Emilia just behind him. They grabbed a bowl to put some water out for Sam. And Springer and Holly could spare a few biscuits.

"What are you two up to?" called Mom, who was weeding her flower beds.

"Nothing," said Kix.

When they were putting the food and water down next to the couch, they spotted Sam. He was out in the field with the horses. There was straw on his coat, and he was walking calmly between Jill and Study and Patriot's legs. Wherever Sam came from, he was obviously used to hooves and horses' teeth.

Kix and Emilia called out, "Sam! Sam!"

And Sam looked up.

They were right. Sam *was* a good name. Otherwise he wouldn't have answered to it.

They held up the water bowl and the dog biscuits, but Sam stayed where he was. It didn't matter, maybe he wasn't thirsty. Maybe he preferred spending more time with Jill and Study and Patriot.

Suddenly all three horses turned their heads. Sam did the same thing — he was looking at the house. And then Kix and Emilia noticed it too — something running toward them. Springer had got out.

Mom shouted, "No, Springer! Here! Here!"

Springer still had to learn to stay in the yard. That was why they kept her inside. Outside she had to stay on the leash.

But now she was loose and galloping happily across the yard. She dashed straight toward the horse pasture, slipped under the wire fence, took a run up and jumped. Onto Sam.

"NO!" Kix screamed. "Springer, STOP!"

Kix and Emilia raced out of the shed, and Mom came running too. "Springer! Springer!"

Springer wanted to play. She snapped at the back of Sam's neck. She slid off his back, careened around him, sniffed his rear end, and clawed the air near his ears with her front paws.

"Springer!" they all called out at the same time. "Springer!"

But Sam wasn't bothered.

He just stood there calmly and — although it was impossible and therefore probably not true, even though they all saw it — smiled calmly at the silly puppy. Then, with one friendly tap of his paw, he laid her down on the ground.

Mom, Kix, and Emilia stood there for a while watching Sam and Springer play with each other. After a few minutes, good old Holly turned up too. She wandered between Sam and Springer's legs, just like Sam had wandered between the horses' legs. It was fun to watch.

Mom put her arms around Kix and Emilia. "Look at that," she said, "three horses, three dogs. And they act like they've known each other for years."

8

Sam kept coming. He would just show up. He did it so quietly that Kix and Emilia would look up and say, "Hey, Sam!"

He surprised them every time because he was always so beautiful and white, and a bit mysterious too.

What did he do when he wasn't with Kix and Emilia? Roam the fields? Or pop back to his actual home across the road? And why didn't the Joneses care that Sam had chosen a different family?

Because that was what had happened. Sam had chosen them. Kix and Emilia had stopped nagging about wanting to keep him, and Dad hadn't said another word about it either. Sam didn't have a collar or a leash. Sam decided for himself when to come and when to go. But he wanted to be petted more and more often, and he slept on the old couch. At night Kix would sometimes hear his *woof!* — a short, raspy bark coming through the darkness to his bedroom. And then Kix was sure of it: Sam didn't come because they wanted to keep *him*. Sam came because *he* wanted to keep *them*.

9

By now Sam would let Kix stroke his back and sides. Emilia sometimes jumped around too much for him, and then Sam would take a small step to the side. But he was always happy for Kix to spread his fingers and slide them through his snow-white hair. Kix loved tracing the path up between Sam's eyes, following it with one finger, then ruffling the hair around Sam's ears, under them and next to them.

Sometimes Sam would growl. That meant he wanted to be petted even more, even harder. And when Kix stopped, Sam would look up at him through the curtain of hair that hung down in front of his eyes. *Don't stop*, said those eyes. And if Kix really had to stop tickling him and telling him what a good boy he was — because Mom was calling or something — then Sam would stand still for a moment. After a while he'd shake his head hard, maybe to get all that hair in place again, maybe because he couldn't believe it was really over.

But Sam didn't like it when people were standing up. Kix and Emilia had to squat down next to him, and he'd only let Mom pet him if she was on the same level as Sam himself, with her hand stretched out as far as possible and saying, "Good boy, good boy."

Dad wasn't home much. He was building an apartment complex in a city that was so far away that he sometimes had to stay there three nights in a row. That's why he didn't see that, for Kix and Emilia, Sam now belonged with the grass, the horses, the house, and them.

10

And then a couple of weeks later, on a Saturday, Kix suddenly heard all kinds of things about Sam.

Grandpa was back from vacation. He and Grandma had been away for three weeks. Grandpa was Mom's dad, but he was also friends with Dad. And now he was drinking a beer on the porch. Grandma was at work.

Emilia was inside watching a movie. Kix was watering the flowers alongside the lawn. He thought he had the best grandpa of anyone he knew and tried to listen to all his stories about the trip. Unfortunately he kept having to move with the hose, so he missed half of it. But then Sam suddenly showed up. He stood on the edge of the lawn and looked at Kix. And now Kix heard what Grandpa said. "Well, what do you know! A Great Pyrenees."

"What?" said Dad.

"Yep, a Pyrenean mountain dog. A purebred. Is he yours? Did you buy him?"

Grandpa knew his dogs. Until recently he'd worked on a ranch, where they'd always had enormous herds of cows and horses, but all kinds of dogs too. Working dogs.

"Well, no," Dad said. "He showed up here a while ago and keeps coming back. He actually belongs to Jones, from across the road, but he seems to think he belongs here with us."

Grandpa stood up. He walked over to Sam, who stared

at the big man and took a slow step backward. Emilia had come outside too, and now she called, "Grandpa, you have to bend over."

Grandpa stopped and looked back in surprise. "Look! Like this," Kix said, showing Grandpa how to avoid scaring Sam.

"For Pete's sake," said Grandpa. But he did go down on one knee.

Slowly, very slowly, Sam came closer — maybe because Kix and Emilia had come over to kneel next to Grandpa.

"Really, a fabulous specimen," said Grandpa, holding out one hand. "But neglected."

Sam stayed where he was, and Grandpa slid over toward him. "Neglected," he said, "and much too submissive."

Neglected? Kix tried to work out what Grandpa meant.

But a little later, when Sam finally began to trust the strange man with the strong hands, Grandpa added, "This dog is way too skinny. Feel these bones . . . he hasn't had a nice time of it."

Kix looked at Grandpa and nodded. It was true. He'd felt that himself, the first time Sam showed up.

Emilia stroked Sam's neck but stayed very, very quiet.

"Grandpa," Kix said, "he wants to stay here with us, because he likes it here. Now he can forget how sad he was."

"Sad?" Grandpa said. "You're probably right. This dog doesn't know what's hit him, getting all this attention. He's been kicked, definitely. There's only a tiny bit of trust left in him."

11

Kix didn't know what to say. Kicked? Had Sam been kicked? All at once he felt a kind of knot in his stomach, and Emilia had a very dark look on her face too.

But there was more nasty news to come.

After all that talk about Sam, Dad suddenly wanted to go over to the Joneses'. Across the road. To talk about Sam. He wanted to go right away, before he forgot about it again.

Grandpa laughed. "You're too late, son. This dog's already made its choice, and the Pyrenees is a stubborn breed."

But Dad said, "I'm going anyway. This is ridiculous — my kids are feeding someone else's dog. I should have gone over earlier. Sarah's even bought an extra bag of dog food."

Sarah was Mom. "I want to go with you," Kix said, even though he thought the neighbors were scary.

"Yes! We're coming too!" Emilia shouted, but Dad wouldn't let them.

Dad went by himself, and it made Kix nervous, because he wasn't sure it was going to turn out well.

But Dad was back after just ten minutes. "How crass can you get?" he grumbled. Kix and Emilia had been waiting for him, standing in front of the horse pasture, as close to the road as possible.

26

"What happened?" Kix asked as he and Emilia followed their father back to the porch. They could hardly keep up with him. And Dad wasn't saying anything. At least not to them.

He walked over to the easy chair next to Mom's and Grandpa's and slumped down on it before sighing, "Okay, it's a sheepdog. For years it guarded a flock of sheep on their oldest son's farm."

"Ah," said Grandpa. He had a strange expression on his face, and he whistled through his teeth. "You mean Flint, I suppose?"

"Yes, the son's name is Flint," Dad said. "Do you know him?"

"Sure do. A difficult guy . . . yes, very difficult . . . but I won't go into that."

"Why is he difficult?" Kix asked. Of course, he and Emilia had come up close to Dad. They didn't want to miss a word.

"Ah . . ." Grandpa shrugged.

"Doesn't matter," Dad said. "Either way, this Flint guy's farm suddenly went bust. About a month ago. Cash-flow problems, over-invested, that kind of thing. He had to get rid of all his sheep and his horses too."

"Oh!" cried Kix. "They were Sam's sheep! And his horses too! Right, Dad?"

"That's right."

"That's why he spends all his time with Jill and Study and Patriot!"

"Does he?" Dad asked. "Anyway, Flint lost his head, a short circuit in the brain, and now he's locked up somewhere."

"What did he do?" Kix asked. "And where's he locked up? In jail?"

What a story! It had Kix on the edge of his seat.

"No," Dad said, "in a kind of hospital. For people with mental disorders."

"And that's why Sam's with them? Across the road? Because Flint's gone all loony?"

"Loony?" Dad said. "That's no way to talk about people."

"Stupid of me," he said to Mom. "I shouldn't have told them. These kids always make up stories about everything."

"Sam is sad!" Emilia started shouting. "Sam is sad, but we're his new friends! And so are our horses!"

"Milly," Mom said, "Sam will get over it."

Kix had been listening to Emilia and Dad, but now he suddenly understood how it all fit together. He wasn't making up a story. He just understood the truth. "Dad . . . Grandpa says Sam was kicked. That was Flint, wasn't it?"

"Dad!" Mom said to Grandpa. "What have you been telling your grandchildren now?"

"You don't have to be an expert to see that, Sarah," Grandpa said. "And the kids have got eyes in their heads. You don't need to protect them from everything."

"But what if that's not what happened?" Mom asked.

And then Grandpa said, "Well . . ."

"What?"

"People say . . ."

"What?" Mom was losing her patience.

"They say that when Flint snapped, he didn't really know what he was doing anymore. He raged and screamed and apparently took a lot of it out on the . . . well, he took it out on the dog . . . eh, I don't know exactly."

"Me neither," Dad said. "But whatever happened, his

parents had him committed. And they didn't know what to do with the dog, so they took it home with them."

The truth — this was the truth. Kix felt the knot in his stomach again. It was square and black. Sam had been through terrible things. Nasty, harsh things that weren't made up.

Now Kix was absolutely certain he would do anything for Sam. So that Sam would never have to go back to that dog-kicker, that Flint. Kix looked at Mom. She was shocked too. She stared down at the grass and the flowers. And she definitely wasn't doing that to make sure Kix had watered them properly.

"So what happens now?" Grandpa asked Dad. "What did they say about your kids and the dog?"

"Huh," growled Dad. "Crass as they come. I tell them, 'That dog's your responsibility. You realize that, don't you? Not ours.' And then the old miser says, 'You can have him for six hundred bucks. He's a purebred.' I say, 'Don't be ridiculous, Jones. We've been feeding him for three weeks now, and I never even said we wanted him!' The old creep just says, 'Whatever. I've got haymaking to do.'"

What had Dad said? Kix couldn't follow it anymore. Did he want to give Sam back? Or not?

Kix was just about to ask for an explanation when Grandpa said, "Ah, don't worry about their hot air. Just give your kids a chance to be kind to that dog."

"Easy for you to say!" Dad snapped. "I'm not going to pay six hundred dollars!"

Kix, and Emilia too, looked from Grandpa to Dad and back again. But then Mom suddenly said, "No, honey, we're not going to pay that. But if Sam wants to come here, that's fine. We're not going to close the gate on him. And anyway, we don't even have a gate."

Everyone laughed, and that seemed to end the afternoon on a good note. Sam came and Sam stayed, Kix understood that now. Because Dad said, "Okay, we'll see."

He wouldn't take Sam back.

But just before they changed the subject, his father said something else. "Oh yeah, before I forget — the dog's not called Sam at all. His name is Nanook."

12

Kix was lying in bed. He stared up at the green stickers of the moon and the planets on his ceiling. They were glowing, because it was nighttime.

Together with Emilia, he'd spent the whole afternoon petting Sam. They'd told him he was safe. And that they were going to look after him forever. That he didn't have to go back to the Joneses. Or their son. And they didn't even mention that horrible name. Flint.

Sam had sat and listened most of the time. But now and then he had walked away. "Doesn't matter," Emilia would say. "He has to pee." Although mostly he didn't pee. If he saw someone coming past on a bike, he'd walk over to the side of the road, bark once or twice, then stroll back. Or else he'd go check on the horses. Or play with Springer. Or leave completely. And after a quarter of an hour, Kix and Emilia would see him again. Then they'd pet him and promise him for the umpteenth time that he was safe. Forever. With them.

And now Kix was lying awake and thinking about Nanook. Nanook didn't even exist. Maybe, if you liked, Nanook could be a hairless granny's dog you'd made up. But Nanook was definitely not a big white fairy-tale dog. How could that awful Flint have given him a name like that? It proved he'd never understood his own dog. Every time Flint called him Nanook, Sam had thought, *I'm not a Nanook, I'm a Sam.*

Kix turned over onto his other side. He still couldn't get to sleep. Because now he was suddenly thinking of sheep. Once, when he was little, Dad put him on a sheep. As a joke, to go for a ride. But the sheep hadn't understood and just lay down. And when they got home Mom could smell it on Kix's pants. "Sheep stink," she said. "We'll still be smelling that twenty years from now."

Kix actually thought sheep were pretty stupid. And he understood why, if you had lots of stupid animals together, you'd need a smart dog to look after them. Sam was a smart dog. He must have been happy running around the flock to keep the sheep together. But he was also strict: he would have barked clearly now and then, once or twice, no more than necessary. Maybe, when an extra dumb sheep didn't understand which way to go, he even nipped it on its heel, just as a warning. And of course Sam would have guarded the flock too and defended it. Against wolves. Against coyotes. And against sheep rustlers. If there was such a thing. Were there sheep rustlers?

Kix wasn't sure.

But when he yawned he suddenly saw little lambs before him. And they, of course, *were* cute. In spring Kix and Emilia and Mom sometimes visited a few sheep farms to see the lambs. And Kix and Emilia were allowed to feed them. You could trick a lamb by dipping your finger in some milk, then it would suck on it and you could feel its soft warm tongue — and its mouth pulled and pulled, quite hard.

Huh? Stupid. Now he had started crying. Out of nowhere. Why now? He didn't like crying, and he was already nine years old.

But then he saw front-end loaders before him. If an animal disease broke out on a farm, they had to kill all the sheep — and the horses too, and the lambs. Because diseases like that are contagious. And Kix had seen it on TV — loaders tipping dead sheep and horses into the backs of trucks. You couldn't imagine anything worse. Yes, there was a knot in Kix's stomach, and he really felt like going to his mother, but Mom and Dad were asleep and he'd wake them up, and what would he say?

Kix didn't go to them, but he kept on crying. Because suddenly he understood what Sam had been through. With his sheep and lambs being taken away from the farm. And the horses too. Isn't that what Mr. and Mrs. Jones had said? Flint had to sell his farm, and all of the animals had to go. That was why Sam was a sad dog. Okay, because his master Loony-Flint had kicked him too, but Sam was a sheepdog without sheep. A horse dog without horses.

No wonder Sam loved Jill and Study and Patriot now. And Emilia and him too. Had Loony-Flint had kids too? No. Otherwise they'd be across the road now. Because Flint was in the hospital for mental cases.

So why had Sam chosen him and Emilia? Did he think they were his sheep?

Kix had to laugh for a moment, between sobs. He yawned again and tried to calm down. He shouldn't think things like this. Maybe they'd just sold the sheep. Without front-end loaders.

He sighed.

Tomorrow he wouldn't let Emilia notice anything. She was too little for all these nasty thoughts. And he would ask Mom if they could buy a bone. For Sam. A nice bone from the pet shop for him to chew on.

13

Did Mom and Dad agree with each other about Sam? Were they both happy for Sam to stay? These were the questions Emilia asked while they were eating pancakes for breakfast.

But she didn't ask Mom and Dad, she asked Kix, and he didn't know either. Dad had already gone to work, and Mom was singing along way too loudly to the country music she always put on when she was in the kitchen.

Kix shrugged. He looked at Emilia. Had she heard him crying last night? He hoped not, because he was her big brother, and big brothers cry as little as possible. He said, "Don't worry. I think Sam's definitely allowed to stay. Dad said so."

"Really?" Emilia smiled.

"Yeah," Kix said. "Last night I heard them talking. I was in bed and I heard Dad say so."

It wasn't true. But Kix was being a real big brother now, and he couldn't imagine them not being allowed to keep Sam.

And to prove it, when Kix asked Mom a little later if they could go to the pet shop to buy a bone for Sam, she just nodded. She said, "That's a good idea. And while we're at it, we'll get a brush too. That long hair of his is one big tangle."

14

Kix could hardly imagine a better shop than their pet shop. He and Emilia had a regular route. First they went to look at the fish. Kix wanted to see the tiger barbs and the black mollies. And the neon tetras, of course. But not the fighting fish — he just felt sorry for them. They were all separate and alone in what looked like jam jars. Then he and Emilia would usually go look at the pet toys. The balls and bells and squeaky mice. And at the end of their tour of the shop, Kix and Emilia always walked over to the big glass cases where they kept the kittens and puppies. Sometimes they had rabbits too. It was a bit smelly with all those animals pooping in the sawdust, but they could still spend hours just looking at them.

And so today Kix and Emilia started on their usual route, but after just fifteen minutes, Mom said, "Sweethearts, we really do need to look for a brush. And maybe Sam should have his own food bowl too?"

"Yes!" cried Kix. He didn't mind at all that they weren't finished looking at the puppies. And Emilia kept quiet too. They found a brush for long hair, then they found a bowl and a fabulous big fat bone. Kix could already imagine Sam running up to get it with his tail wagging.

"Mom," Kix said, "I can't wait to get home. Can we go now?"

They left right away, but in the parking lot Mom turned

around to face them in the back seat and said, "I want you to listen carefully to what I have to say."

"Okay, Mom," said Emilia. Kix didn't say anything.

"Your father is having trouble deciding about Sam. We're definitely not going to buy Sam from the Joneses, and I don't think we need to. That six hundred dollars was probably a joke. But to be honest about it, Sam still officially belongs to them, even if Dad and I say he can stay."

Kix sniffed. He said, "Sam chose us himself."

"Yes," Mom said, "he did. But I want you to think about the situation as it is now. I mean, if we look after Sam and he keeps sleeping in our shed, and if we all start to love him very much, then we still don't know what will happen if Sam wants to go back one day."

"I love Sam very, very, very much!" Emilia shouted. "Already!"

Mom smiled, "I know you do."

"Mom," Kix asked, "do you mean if Loony-Flint comes back?"

"He's called Flint, Kix. Not Loony-Flint."

"Loony-Flint!" Emilia laughed. "Loony-Flint! Ha-ha-ha!"

"Kix! Emilia!" Mom warned, "we don't call *anyone* loony. People who are sick are sick. Whether it's in their stomach or in their head."

"Well," said Kix, "then I'll call him Sick-Flint."

Emilia laughed again. But Kix didn't think it was fair of Mom to start talking about Flint again and Sam wanting to go back to Flint, because Flint had kicked him and beaten him. "Sam chose us," Kix said again. "That's all there is to it, Mom. And why did you have to go and ruin my mood?"

Mom reached over from the front seat and touched his cheek. "I'm sorry, sweetie. You're right. Sam *has* chosen us. And that's why we have to think it through. Sam's the one who decides what happens. Sheepdogs are loyal, and if Sam decides to go back to his master, that's his decision too. We'll look after him as best we can. We'll try to make him forget how sad he was. But Sam's the boss. Not us."

15

During the drive home, Kix was thinking. About Sam and about what his mother had said. *Stupid Mom*, he thought. *Stupid Mom for being right.*

Of course Kix knew they couldn't keep Sam if Sam didn't want them to. Sam didn't even have a collar. How was Kix supposed to hold on to Sam if he wanted to go back to Loony-Flint? Wrap his arms around him, and lie on top of him? That would be as pointless as climbing on a sheep's back. Sam would run out from under him, and Kix would fall smack on the ground. Yes, stupid Mom, because now he was stuck on the stupid back seat of the car with stupid thoughts in his head.

But here was their road. And in the distance Kix could already see what he was searching for — a warm, soft, white spot. That was Sam, it couldn't be anything else. Sam, their very own fairy-tale ghost dog.

16

But something was up. Something strange.

Lying down next to Sam, who was standing up straight, was another white dog. A smaller one, with short hair, but also a kind of fairy-tale ghost dog.

For a moment, Kix thought, *Are there more of them? Is Sam the boss of a whole parade of white dogs?* Maybe it wasn't a ghost world, but a fairy-tale land with a fairy-tale flock? No — he was dreaming. And he'd just turned nine, so all those made-up thoughts were silly. How could he be so childish?

And then Emilia suddenly started screaming. "Blood, Mom! That other dog's got blood! That other dog is dead!"

Mom slammed on the brakes and spun around to face them. "You two stay in the car!"

She got out, slamming the door behind her.

Kix stared out of the side window. The second white dog was still lying on the ground, not far from the field. There was a red patch on its neck that could only be blood. It was terrible — it was horrible! But then Kix saw something much more horrible: there was blood on Sam too. On his mouth. There was blood on Sam's jaws.

"Sam!" Mom shouted. She was walking more stiffly than usual, and her voice was loud and angry.

Sam killed that dog, thought Kix. The words raced through his head: *Sam killed that dog.*

But then the smaller dog got up.

"Sam!" Mom shouted again. And then she went "Shoo!" at the strange dog.

Kix really didn't understand what was going on, but he couldn't just stay sitting in the car. He unclicked his seat belt, climbed over to the front, and pointed at Emilia just like Mom had. "You stay there!"

Then he jumped out.

He ran over to Mom. *Sam hadn't killed the strange dog after all. The strange dog wasn't dead.* But as Kix ran over, others were running too. Springer thrummed past. How had she gotten loose? Had Dad come home? Yes, Dad was home — Kix could see his pickup truck.

Springer sprinted over to the new dog. She wanted to play, Springer always wanted to play. She sped up and already had a happy front paw up in the air.

Kix and Mom called out to her, but she didn't hear them.

Emilia called out too. Of course she had climbed out of the car just like Kix.

The new dog looked up, and Springer jumped on it happily. "Nooo!" shouted Kix and Mom and Emilia, "SPRINGER!"

But it was already too late.

For a moment the new dog stood there — motionless, surprised. It didn't mind Springer wanting to touch it and sniff it from all sides, or maybe it hadn't really figured out what was happening. Because it bent its head to sniff Springer too — and then Sam was there.

With one blow, Sam knocked the new dog over again.

Sam snarled and barked, and the new dog squealed and whimpered. Sam forced it roughly onto its back with his hard paws. Sam snapped at it and bit it.

And everyone watching the fighting dogs could see that Sam was a mean dog.

Kix and Emilia didn't move. Or maybe they did — they couldn't remember afterwards because of the fright Mom gave them. She screamed.

Sam looked up. For a second he stopped growling and snapping.

That was enough for the strange dog. Quick as a flash it wriggled free and fled with its tail tucked down between its legs. To the road. Headed for town.

Things went very quiet. Kix, Emilia, and Mom were standing in a semicircle around Sam. They were panting.

But Sam was panting even harder. His tongue was flopping around outside his mouth, and threads of slime were hanging from his jaws. He looked up through the hair over

42

his eyes, all sweet and shy again, as if he'd never been a different kind of dog.

Emilia started crying.

Kix felt like crying too, but he was still frozen, and there was only one thought in his head: Sam had just been a different kind of dog.

A dog that attacked other dogs.

A dog that wanted to be the boss.

A horrible dog.

17

Mom comforted Emilia.

Sam realized that he wasn't going to be petted right now and shuffled off to the horses. Springer had spotted a few pigeons that needed to be chased out of a tree.

Kix still didn't understand exactly what had happened. But walking along behind Mom and Emilia, he knew that nothing was going to be the same again. Sam wasn't a fairy-tale ghost dog anymore, sad and sorrowful. And it wasn't right to pick out beautiful brushes and delicious bones for him. They could take them right back to the shop, because Sam was a monster. A nightmare dog, that was what he was.

Mom made some pink lemonade for Emilia in the kitchen. She was talking with a calm voice again. She was talking about canine behavior and tails between legs, but Kix didn't want to hear it.

He went into the living room.

There was Dad. Lying on the couch. He was just waking up from an afternoon nap and said, "Oowaaah . . . I think I nodded off. Did I miss anything?"

And then Kix knew that it would all come out, how bloodthirsty Sam had been, and then Dad would chase Sam away.

Away.

Forever.

18

Just when Mom was about to tell Dad about Sam biting the other dog, they heard a pickup on the driveway. Grandpa!

And a little later they were all sitting around the kitchen table. Emilia and Kix with lemonade, Mom and Grandpa and Dad with cans of beer — Kix had pulled off the tabs for them.

Dad and Grandpa heard what had happened with Sam and the strange dog, and Kix kept his eyes on Dad's face. Any moment now Dad was going to say that enough was enough. That he'd never wanted a third dog. That he was going straight to the Joneses, and they'd take Sam back to Loony-Flint, and maybe that was where he belonged anyway. Because Sam had gone a bit crazy too.

But something completely different happened.

Grandpa started to laugh.

He slapped Dad on the back with his big hand. "Way to go!" he said. "You've got yourself a watchdog!"

Kix's jaw dropped. He stared at Grandpa with big eyes. Was Sam a watchdog? Had Sam done the right thing?

Grandpa laughed again. And now Dad laughed along with him. "Yeah," he said, "you've got a point."

And Mom? Kix looked at Mom.

"There's one thing I'm sure of," she said, looking at Dad. "If you have to spend another night or two away for work, we'll sleep a lot safer."

"Yeah," Dad said again, "you've got a point there."

Kix thought and thought. Maybe the fourth dog was an intruder? A dog that deserved to be bitten?

And then Grandpa spoke to him and Emilia, "You're lucky to have a dog like Sam. He was a sheepdog, you see. And he watched over a herd. Your father should see it like this: Sam's found a new herd, and that's you and the horses and Holly and Springer. And you can bet he'll watch over you too."

19

Normally Kix had at least twenty tricks to stay up later than he was supposed to. Emilia wasn't bad at it either. Whining, making up excuses, asking for an extra chapter of one of their favorite books. From the series about the pig who wants to be a fireman or the adventures of Captain Underpants. But tonight Emilia fell asleep right away. Kix could hear her snoring, he really could — it was very quiet girl-snoring, but it still came right through the wall between her bedroom and his. And he couldn't stop yawning either.

During dinner and dessert and watching TV afterwards, he hadn't been able to think about anything except Sam. He'd wanted to go out to check on him, but Mom said it was too late. And that Sam was out in the middle of the field with Jill and Study and Patriot. "Bedtime for you," she said, and Kix didn't mind.

He didn't complain, and within a minute he was sound asleep.

But in the middle of the night a strange, high-pitched noise woke him up.

For a moment Kix didn't know where he was — oh, that's right — in bed, of course.

The noise sounded sad, but where was it coming from? What was it?

Kix sat up straight and stayed as quiet as possible. Then he figured it out: the noise was coming from Sam. It was Sam howling. Like a wolf. Sometimes he would be quiet for a moment, but then Sam would start again: long and drawn out and lonely. Kix threw off his quilt. He put his feet down on the rug. He straightened his pajama top, which had crept up while he was asleep.

He walked over to his bedroom door.

Why was Sam howling? Was he just sad, or was he calling someone?

Kix had to go to him. He didn't think about whether he was allowed to or not. He just pulled open his bedroom door and slipped out into the hall. *Sam,* he thought, *Sam, Sam . . .*

Was Emilia awake? No. Kix could still hear her softly snoring.

His dog howled again, a very long howl this time, and Kix left Emilia to sleep. *Sam,* he thought, *Sam, Sam!* He ran to the laundry room, then through to the garage — he saw that Holly and Springer were awake, but he was in a hurry. He slipped his boots on and opened the door to the yard.

The night hadn't gotten cold yet, but it was dark. The only light was the one in the stable, and next to that was Sam's old shed. Kix hurried over the gravel, past the pile of sand and the old boards Dad had left outside.

"Sam?" Kix said. Sam wasn't howling anymore, and there weren't any other noises either. Maybe Springer and Holly had gone back to sleep. "Sam?"

Kix had made it to the shed. He stood still for a moment to let his eyes adjust to the darkness. There, in the back, he could see a white mountain. On the old couch.

The white mountain looked up.

"Sam?" Kix whispered.

Suddenly Mom was there too.

She laid her hands on his shoulders and pulled him back against her. "Hey," she said, "you know we don't do that. Sneaking out at night."

"Sam was howling," Kix said.

"I know," Mom said. "I heard it too. Is that why you came outside?"

"I thought he was sad. I thought he wanted to say something."

Mom said, "Kix . . ."

Now a creaking noise came from the back of the shed. And a shuffling sound. The white mountain waddled out, and of course it was Sam. Who wanted to be petted, even though it was the middle of the night.

"Just a few minutes, Kix," Mom said, "and then we're going back inside."

Kix knelt down and held out his hand. Sam stepped up and ran his coat along Kix's hand as if to show him where to pet.

"Kix," Mom said, while Kix rubbed his hands back and forth over Sam's soft white coat, "when dogs howl, they're not sad. Dogs howl because they hear a sound. And that sound has a particular frequency that sets them off. When they hear it, they have to make noise too. Sam heard the trains. The trains on the track past our field. They always blow their horns at night. To make sure nobody drives onto the tracks. As a warning. We don't even notice it anymore, we're that used to it. But not Sam. That's why he howls."

"Oh," said Kix.

He kept petting Sam, and Sam hadn't had enough of it yet. There was still some blood around his mouth, but it wasn't that red anymore.

"Come on, honey," Mom said. "Everything's fine. Let's go."

"Hmm," said Kix.

And finally he had to let go. Train noises. Warnings. High frequencies. Hmm. Maybe Mom was right.

They walked back, and once again Mom told him that he wasn't allowed to go out at night. That she understood him doing it, after all that had happened today. But he had to promise never to do it again.

Kix promised. He was tired enough to go back to bed anyway. But at the same time he knew that Sam had howled about something else. Not about the trains. Sam had howled because he was sorry. Kix had seen it in his eyes when he was petting him. *Sorry*, those eyes said. *Sorry I upset you so much today, Kix.*

20

At first Sam thought the brush was weird. But Kix and Emilia used long, even strokes on the side of his body and kept saying, "Good boy, strong boy," and after a while he probably thought, *Oh, this is like being petted. Nice.* And then he stood up so that Kix and Emilia could easily brush his whole body from top to bottom.

Emilia sang a song, Kix laughed, and every now and then Sam gave a very deep sigh.

After just three strokes the brush was completely full of loose hair. Kix plucked the balls of white out and threw them away. The tufts blew around on the ground, and after an hour it looked like it had been snowing little clouds of hair.

Mom came to have a look and said, "Dogs like this should actually be brushed twice a week."

"How do you know that?" Kix asked.

"I looked it up," Mom said, "on the internet. Sam's a mountain dog. Mountain dogs are outside dogs. They have a good tolerance for cold and a good tolerance for heat. But they need to get rid of their loose hair now and then."

"Look!" Emilia cried. "Sam says you're right. He's nodding!"

It was true — Sam was moving his head up and down. "That's just a coincidence," Kix said. But of course it wasn't that coincidental. Kix understood perfectly what Sam was saying: *Keep brushing, you. And twice a week isn't nearly enough.*

21

Sam was addicted to being petted. Kix had figured that out by now and would sneak off to the open shed as often as he could. To look for Sam. So he could say hello and tickle Sam between the eyes. Or under his left ear. That was Sam's favorite spot. If you did it properly, his hind leg started to shake in time.

Kix always put some dog food in Sam's bowl. Mom said he was only allowed to do it once a day, but you could still feel how skinny Sam was under all that hair, so a little extra food wasn't going to do him any harm.

Anyway — although Sam ate the food, he didn't actually think it was that important. When you fed Holly and Springer, they pushed your hands and legs out of the way in their rush to get at the bowl. Sam always waited until Kix had walked off. Until he had stopped looking back. He wanted to be sure he wasn't going to be petted anymore first.

Dad had noticed it too. He even said, "Sam is the only dog in the world who loves attention more than food."

A couple of days later Kix and Mom found out something else special about Sam. He patrolled. That's what Mom called it. He made his rounds. A couple of times a day they saw him doing a circuit of their property. He would march out to the far side of the horse pasture, then go behind the stable, behind the old shed and the garage, behind the house, and finish his round past Mom's garden and Dad's cornfield. He'd end up at the end of the yard near the road, where he would sniff the air for a while and then, if everything was good and safe, lumber back to his spot near the planks, or go into the field, or come over to someone who was luring him with an open hand.

Sam patrolled, that was what it was called. Sam checked the surroundings. Sam was a soldier.

But he seemed happiest when Mom went riding.

Mom had once ridden races on Patriot, and she went riding a couple of times a week, mostly out past the fields late in the afternoon. Sometimes she rode alone, sometimes Kix rode next to her on Study, because Study never bucked, and she did everything Patriot did.

When Sam saw Mom lifting the saddle down from the stable wall, he'd start to run circles in the straw and slip in and out between the horses' legs. And when they went out onto the road, he'd trot alongside. Wherever they went and however long they stayed out, Sam would run next to them. He kept an eye on them and wagged his tail cheerfully in the wind.

"Honey," Mom said to Dad one evening, "if anything ever goes wrong on a ride, if Patriot goes lame and I'm lying in a ditch, Sam will come get you. I'm sure of it."

22

The weeks passed, and everyone was used to Sam. He barked when strangers drove into the yard — as a warning — but he didn't bite anyone, and there was no more blood. He backed off as soon as he saw that Mom or Dad or Kix or Emilia was walking up to the strangers.

Grandpa had been right. They had themselves a watchdog. But only when necessary.

Sometimes Kix still heard Sam barking at night or howling, and Mom was right — he did it when the train was blowing its horn before the bend.

And Sam understood why Kix loved Grandpa so much. Sam loved Grandpa too. He still wouldn't walk up to grownups, especially if they were standing up straight and stayed

standing. But nowadays, when Dad and Grandpa were having a beer on the lawn, Sam would quietly sneak up behind their chairs. Especially Grandpa's. And when Grandpa said what he always said, "A magnificent creature!" Sam would slide his head in under Grandpa's hand.

"A magnificent creature!" Grandpa would say again, but this time to Dad. "You got lucky there."

And Dad would grumble something in reply.

But he would smile too. Kix had seen him do it a couple of times.

Sam was Sam. And that made everyone happy.

23

And then that thing with Springer happened.

It was a hot afternoon, and Dad went off to check on his new field. It was behind the horse pasture, and Dad had bought it so he could build a house for Grandma and Grandpa on it later. But first he was going to grow grass on it, because he could use that to make hay for the horses.

Springer loved that field. She tore across it from left to right and from right to left. She chased rabbits and birds, and when there weren't any, she chased clouds instead.

Sometimes Sam stood on the side of the field watching Springer. But on that one hot afternoon he decided to run around with her. Mom had taken Emilia to her swimming lesson, and Kix and Dad stared at a small speedy brown spot racing along in the distance (Springer) and a slow white one trundling along behind (Sam). "Just look at those two," Dad said.

"Yeah," Kix said, "Sam's a good runner too. Sam isn't old at all."

"Hmm, I make him about ten or so," Dad said. "Oh, look, they've found some crows."

And so they had. Springer went swish-swish-swish, and Sam followed her, bound-bound-bound, chasing the angry flock. Dad and Kix could hardly even hear their happy barking, that's how far away Springer and Sam were now.

"They'd better not go on the road," Dad said.

But that was exactly what they did.

Dad stuck his fingers in his mouth and whistled loudly. He was training Springer to be more obedient, and whistling usually helped. Usually Springer came running back right away when he called her like that. With little detours, of course. Springer couldn't run anywhere in a straight line. But now Springer wasn't listening at all. She was almost out of sight.

Sam did come lurching back to Kix and Dad. He dropped down on his stomach in front of them and looked up as if he was ashamed of himself.

"Don't worry, Sam," Kix said, "nobody can keep up with Springer. And you're already ten."

"Come on," Dad said, "we'll take the truck. Springer must have gone off after a couple of cyclists or something."

They left Sam behind with the horses and took the pickup, driving around the field once, then coming back in the opposite direction. Dad searched and Kix searched, but they couldn't see Springer anywhere. Finally Dad said, "Maybe she ran back home through the fields by herself."

They weren't really worried. Outside of town there wasn't much traffic, and the local farmers didn't drive fast anyway. But just when they were about to turn into their driveway, they saw an angry man on the road. He gestured at them and shouted, "Hey! What's the idea? That dog of yours is at my place now!"

It didn't sound friendly at all, and the man from across the road didn't *look* friendly either. Because that was who was standing there shouting. Mr. Jones from across the road.

24

Dad stopped in the middle of the road, jumped out, and said, "Hi, there!"

"That yappy little mutt of yours!" screamed Mr. Jones.

"Calm down, Buck," Dad said. Apparently Buck was Mr. Jones's first name. From inside the car, Kix watched the wound-up, angry gestures of the man who had once owned a snake. Kix definitely hadn't forgotten that. A python. As a pet.

"Calm down?" Mr. Jones shouted. "I wish that stupid dog of yours would calm down for once! Chickens running in all directions. I'm standing there painting creosote on the coop, and the little monster comes jumping around my legs, the creosote tips over, all down my pants, that stuff stinks to high heaven, and you're paying for a new can, okay?"

"Okay," said Dad. "Sure. I've got some left somewhere. Where's Springer now? Did you tie her up?"

"Why the hell should I! And I don't want an old can. I want a new can, and you can pay for my pants too. And in the future keep that damn mutt at your place!"

Ooh, thought Kix. *Swearing. Dad doesn't like that. Ooh, now Dad's going to get angry.* And he was right. He saw Springer suddenly shoot out from behind Mr. Jones's shed and run back home. But he also saw Dad plant his boots firmer on the ground and say, "Buck! Did I hear you right?

You say I should keep my dog at my place? And you're serious, eh? And you've conveniently forgotten about the discussion we've had a couple of times now. About your dog being on my land for weeks now, with my horses and my kids? And me feeding it, when it's your, I repeat, *your* dog."

No, Dad, thought Kix, *don't say that. Next thing Mr. Jones will want . . . Mr. Jones will say . . .* And Kix was right again. Because Mr. Jones was already saying it. He stepped

closer to Dad. He poked Dad in the chest with one finger and said, "Now you mention it. Six hundred dollars. It's a purebred dog. So you can't just keep it, like you're trying to."

"What?" Dad shouted, pushing the finger away. "I'm not trying to do anything! And I'm not paying anything either! You let him go! You haven't made any attempt to get him back!"

"Oh no?" Mr. Jones said. He was wavering now, Kix could tell.

"No," Dad said.

Suddenly it was as if Mr. Jones had lost all his anger. As if he'd forgotten how to scream and shout.

"Ah, man," he said. "Fine, whatever. I'll come and get Nanook. You just make sure I can creosote my coop."

Kix felt cold all of a sudden. Get Nanook? Nanook was Sam! And Sam was his and Emilia's. Had Dad forgotten that?

But Dad didn't even object. He just said, "Okay, Buck. That's settled then."

And he held out his hand.

And Mr. Jones shook that hand.

25

Of course Kix was angry. At Dad. And at Mr. Jones. But Dad said, "Kixie, do you really think Mr. Jones wants to come and get Sam back? If he did, he would have done it ages ago. Really, it was all hot air. Come on, we'll take him a can of that stuff, we'll keep Springer tied up, and nothing will change."

Kix let himself be reassured. When Dad said something it was usually true. Dad understood people. "Mr. Jones is an old grump, Kix. People like that need to grumble, it's all they've got."

But within a day of Springer disappearing, Mr. and Mrs. Jones suddenly appeared next to Sam's open shed. Kix didn't see it, and neither did Emilia — they'd gone to play at Grandma and Grandpa's. They only heard about it when they got home. Mom told them that the Joneses hadn't given up easily. "Na-nook!" they'd called. "Naaaa-NOOK!" And Sam had looked up, briefly, but definitely wasn't going to do what they said. They'd tried to lure him with bones and balls, and they'd even used Springer, borrowing her for a while. And Sam had gone with them for a minute or two, before ambling back home again. To their house — Kix's and his and Mom's and Emilia's and everyone else's.

So yes, Dad was right. Everything stayed the same.

Kix's heart had started to pound nervously when he heard that they really had tried to take Sam, but Sam was still there. Sam still wanted to be petted, and Sam's tail was wagging more and more cheerfully, higher and higher in the air. Especially when he saw Kix.

Until that evening came.

That terrible evening.

That evening Mom read three whole chapters of *Captain Underpants*. Then she left him after a kiss and a cuddle like always. But then Kix suddenly heard a noise outside in the yard. He jumped up out of bed and ran to the kitchen window. Dad was outside. Mom too. There were lights and barking.

Kix didn't know what was going on. But then Mom came in. And she was holding a hand up to her eyes.

"What's wrong?" Kix asked. "Mom, what's wrong?"

Mom started to cry. That was something she almost never did. Kix walked over to her. He felt dizzy. He knew before he heard it that something terrible had happened.

"He's gone, Kix," Mom said. "This time they've really taken him. Across the road. Our Sam."

26

When Kix got angry, really angry, he felt it inside his head. Mom called it a pressure cooker hissing and bubbling inside of him, and it made Kix's thoughts glow red-hot, and his forehead glowed too.

Mostly Kix would go to his room and punch one of his stuffed animals. There was nothing wrong with that, it didn't hurt them, and they even understood. After a while Kix calmed down again and the pressure cooker was gone.

But not tonight. Now Kix felt something he'd never felt before. Not a hot pressure cooker, no, but something cold. A block of ice, maybe. A frozen block in his stomach.

Dad came back home, and Kix could only stare at him. Kix stood in the middle of the living room.

Dad walked up to him.

Dad squatted down in front of him. He took hold of Kix with both hands, but Kix broke free.

"Kixie," Dad said, "don't worry. They thought it might be easier at night. They'll keep him there tonight, sure, but tomorrow Sam will come skipping back across the road."

Skipping? thought Kix. *Sam doesn't skip. Sam never skips. Dad used the wrong word. Dad doesn't know Sam. And if he doesn't know Sam, how can he be so sure Sam will come back?*

He felt bad. It was partly because of that cold ice inside

68

of him, but mostly because of something he had just realized: *Dad's just saying that.*

Maybe Dad hoped that Sam would come back, but he didn't know it for sure. This time Dad wasn't right. This time Dad didn't have any say in it — the Joneses could do whatever they liked.

And Dad was just saying that.

To him, to his own son. And it was about Sam, who had gentle eyes and gentle thoughts and would always be treated gently by Kix and everyone else. Except by the Joneses of course. They'd kick him. Maybe even tonight. They had a son who was crazy, and if your son's crazy maybe you're not completely normal yourself.

So how could Dad —

Suddenly it happened. All that hard ice inside him shot into Kix's elbows. He pushed against Dad's shoulders.

And since Dad was squatting down, Dad fell over.

Dad sprawled on the ground. Kix was shocked, but he knew he'd done it on purpose.

"Kix!" Mom cried.

Kix turned to look at her. Her eyes were still red. And Mom wouldn't cry for no reason. She knew that Sam —

Dad grabbed him. He picked Kix up, threw him over his shoulder, and carried him to his bedroom door in three furious steps. "Jason!" Mom shouted at Dad, but he had already set Kix down hard on the bed.

"NOT ANOTHER WORD!" Dad shouted, loud and clear. "You close your eyes and go to sleep and you just trust your father!"

After that Dad stormed off. He whacked the switch next to the door to turn off the light, but it went on instead,

because it hadn't been on to start with. He immediately whacked it a second time, and the light flicked off.

"If I say it will work out . . ." Dad began, speaking to the darkness, speaking to Kix, but he didn't finish his sentence.

Instead he turned and walked out.

The door slammed shut behind him.

For a moment there was silence. Then came the sound of crying from Emilia's room.

She was upset, of course. But Kix didn't hear that anymore, because he had grabbed his pillow and pressed it against his mouth, and now he was screaming into it. Long and loud, with ice-cold, frozen anger.

27

Kix woke up and his head hurt.

It was the middle of the night, and everyone was in bed. There was no more sound from the living room.

After Dad's outburst, Kix had screamed even more. He had cried too. Mom had come, but he didn't want to talk to her either. Then he cried some more. After that he'd probably fallen asleep.

And now it was dark, inside and out.

The headache might have come from crying. Or from being angry.

In the old days, Kix always crawled under the couch when someone was angry. The anger was a lot thinner under there. You could still hear the angry words, but they flew over you. When the air was clear again, he'd crawl back out from his hiding place.

Nowadays he didn't fit under the couch. He didn't want to either. He didn't want to hide anymore.

That was weird because Kix still hated it when people got angry. But now it was about Sam, and this time it was serious.

Kix shook his head. Maybe he was so sure about it because he loved Sam more than the others did. More than Mom and more than Emilia too. Was that it?

Kix shook his head again.

And then he heard the train.

Too-oooot. It was a warning for the railroad crossing, like always at night.

Too-oooot. Too-oooot.

And a little later that other sound went up in the night: Sam's howl.

But Sam's howl sounded quieter. It was coming from all the way across the road. It sounded sadder too. More like he was calling out to him, Kix. More helpless.

Kix's headache was gone. Disappeared, from one second to the next.

That might have been because Kix was suddenly sure of one other thing: that Dad wouldn't get up. Dad still believed that everything was going to work out. Kix knew that Mom wouldn't get up either, because Mom believed what Dad believed. Nobody would get up, because nobody heard and felt what Kix heard and felt.

So Kix had to do it himself.

Kix had to get up.

He had to go through the night to get to Sam.

28

Kix pulled on his socks and his slippers.

The last time Kix went outside in the dark, Mom had heard him. She'd followed him. He'd made too much noise, of course.

This time he wouldn't do that.

Kix found a sweatshirt on the floor — that was warm enough. Everything he did, he did very slowly, and he listened to two things at once. To himself, to make sure he wasn't being too noisy. And to the rest of the house, to hear if there was any other movement.

Holly and Springer were in their baskets in the garage. Last time Kix had woken them up, and they probably woke Mom. This time Kix wouldn't go through the garage, but through the living room and out the front door.

Off he went.

He stepped into the hallway and walked past Emilia's door.

Should he wake her up?

Sam was her dog too, of course. And maybe she loved Sam just as much as he did. She'd given Sam his name. And they'd found him together.

Kix laid his hand on her doorknob. He turned it softly — then stopped. Emilia was his little sister. He was her big brother. What if something horrible happened to Sam? What if something went wrong? If Sam —

No, he had to do this by himself.

Kix felt cold all of a sudden. But he crept on. Cold and silent, he crept through the living room.

Through the front door.

Past Mom's flowers.

Down the driveway.

29

Kix stopped at the side of the road, but of course that wasn't necessary. Who was going to be driving past in the middle of the night? Nobody. Kix stood there all alone.

He looked back for a moment. At the house.

Mom, Dad, Emilia, Holly, Springer — they were all still asleep. The horses were standing on the far side of the field. Maybe they were awake, maybe not.

He knew Sam was on the other side of the road. "Sam," Kix whispered, almost without making a sound. He crossed the road and looked at Mr. and Mrs. Jones's driveway. He mustn't wake them up. He mustn't wake up anyone except Sam. Kix would find him and take him back home, and maybe it would all be over in a couple of minutes.

Kix was glad that he had his slippers on and not his mud boots. Or his cowboy boots. The soft soles of his slippers didn't make any noise at all on the gravel driveway.

Kix didn't know exactly where to go, and he was too scared to call Sam. But he was sure he'd be heading back again in no time. Two or three minutes, that was all. And by now his eyes were used to the night, so it wasn't even that dark.

The Joneses' house was on one side of the gravel driveway, and the shed was on the other. Kix was walking down that side of the drive. He knew that some houses had outside lights that flashed on when you walked past. They were usually above the front door. Or the kitchen door. So those were places he had to avoid.

Kix stopped in front of the shed door and listened. When he got up, just a few minutes ago, he hadn't thought about how he would find Sam. For a moment he saw the image that got stuck in his head a while back: Sam trapped in a glass box. That was nonsense, of course. How could he have ever come up with something like that? Back then he still believed in fairy-tale dogs. But now he was sneaking through the yard of the people who had stolen Sam away and stuffed him into a cage in the shed or put him on a nasty chain, and it was nighttime and not that cold, but it was definitely real.

Kix's heart said so too. That this was real. It was pounding high in his chest.

He crept on, staying close to the shed. "Sam," he whispered softly . . . where had they put him?

It was almost like the sound of his breathing: "Sam . . . Sam . . . Sam . . ."

Two or three minutes, that was all it would take. Maybe four.

Kix had come to the end of the shed. He hadn't heard anything moving inside. Maybe he had to go back to the door and try to open it? Or wait — he was so stupid! He'd heard Sam howl before. That meant that Sam couldn't possibly be inside somewhere.

Three or four minutes. Five at most.

Behind the shed there was a lawn. That lawn was like a big dark square. There were no jump ropes on it, like at home, no badminton set, no scooters. It was wide and dark green. Along the sides were black bushes.

"Sam?" Kix said. "Sam?"

And then he saw it. Something white rising to its feet at the end of the green-black field. Something white that was making a snuffling noise.

Kix ran over as fast as he could. Now he could see it better. Yes, it was Sam. But there was chicken wire too. Sam was locked up in an old chicken run. He tried to stand up straight and stretch himself, but he couldn't because the cage was too low.

"Sam! Sam! Sam!" Kix said. He didn't care anymore whether anyone heard him. He had come here to set Sam free. It would only take another two minutes or so. Maybe just one.

Kix ran his fingers over the chicken wire in search of the door. It wasn't at the front, but where? Left . . . right . . . Yes, right. He tugged on it, but there was a wooden latch. He slid it open. "Sam! Sam! Sam!"

Sam looked at him. He stood there waiting with his back pushed up against the top of the pen.

"Come on, Sam!" Kix said, but then he suddenly realized what he had to do. He had to clear the way. He had to open the door, go a bit further away, and crouch down. Squatting on his heels.

Kix did all of that. He squatted down about ten feet from the cage and held out his hand.

Slowly, Sam crept out of the run. The first thing he did when he was all the way out was give himself a good shake. Then he lowered his head and walked, walked right to Kix. And he rubbed, pushed, and forced the side of his head against Kix's fingers.

Three minutes, two, one minute — Kix had promised himself he'd leave this yard as quickly as possible, just grab Sam and go. But now that he felt Sam's soft white coat again, he couldn't do anything except pet him. He rubbed all that warm cascading hair, under Sam's chin and around Sam's ears, and Sam wanted more and harder and more, and Kix wanted more and harder and more.

Kix pressed his nose against Sam, and Sam let him do it.

Kix wrapped his arms around Sam's neck, and Sam let him do that too.

"Sammy," Kix whispered into Sam's ear, "you coming? You belong with us, don't you?"

And then he froze.

Because he saw a red light.

Just ten or so feet further along, a red light glowed on and then off again.

It took Kix a couple of seconds to figure out that the light was from a cigarette. With a person behind it.

Someone was standing there smoking.

Kix was still too shocked to move and Sam, too, was staring at the man, because that was what it was — a man.

Kix didn't know him. The man was younger than Mr. Jones, but when the red light glowed again, Kix saw that he looked like Mr. Jones.

And he had a gun.

Kix could see that clearly now.

There was a rifle hanging from the man's shoulder. On a strap.

And because of Sam, Kix suddenly realized who it was, the man with the gun who was standing there looking at

them. Sam started to wag his tail. Very slowly, very cautiously. This man was someone Sam knew.

And that meant there was only one person it could be. Loony-Flint.

Kix was getting a cramp. He had to stand up, and that meant letting go of Sam as well. Sam took a step to the side, like he always did when someone near him stood up.

Kix's fingers suddenly felt cold. And so did his toes. They were cold too. All at once. Because of the slippers. They were too thin. Kix felt cold all over. Cold and tense.

Next to him, Sam was still slowly wagging his tail. That was the worst thing.

That, and the gun.

30

Flint, the man, just stood there.

Smoking.

Kix stood there too. All he could do was wait and see what would happen.

Flint took a drag on his cigarette. The cigarette flashed a red signal. He held his smoky breath and then, after a while, blew it out again — a stream that started fast and straight but soon dissolved into the night.

It wasn't until the cigarette was nothing but a stub that Flint said something: "A kid."

His voice sounded strange, like he wasn't used to using it. There was a crack in it too, something broken.

"Mr. Flint," Kix said. He didn't know what else to say.

"Huh," the man said.

He did something complicated with his fingers that made the last bit of the cigarette fly off. It arced through the air and landed in the grass.

"You know who I am," Flint said, "and you've got my dog."

Kix didn't answer. He still didn't know what needed to be said, and he couldn't manage it anyway. Kix kept staring at the gun. His eyes kept going back to it.

"Ha," the man said. "I'm not going to shoot you or anything."

Then something nasty happened.

Kix had needed to pee for a while now, and he couldn't hold back any longer. He squeezed and squeezed but still felt the warmth on his thighs. A wet spot appeared on his pajama bottoms and slowly spread. Kix felt so incredibly stupid there in the cold, in the night — it made him furious.

And suddenly he could talk again. "I," he said, "I'm angry."

Flint started to laugh. It was a horrible laugh. "Angry?" he said. "You? If you ask me, you need to go beddy-bye."

"And you . . . you shouldn't be in the hospital — you should be in jail!"

Flint laughed again, but this time he kept it short.

"Wow," he said, "you're a brave one."

He slid his rifle aside and got something out of his pocket. A lighter. And a pack of cigarettes.

He shook it carefully until a new cigarette appeared. Then lit it, put the pack back in his coat pocket, and took a drag on it. Only then did he start talking again. Smoke poured out of his mouth as he spoke, "And why should I be in jail, according to you?"

Sam was still standing next to Kix. Now and then he looked to the side, at the bushes, before turning his head back to Kix or Flint. His tail was drooping.

Kix felt the warm, wet spot between his legs start to cool off. But he was still angry. "Because of you, your sheep and horses went bust, everyone says so, and maybe there wasn't a front-end loader or maybe there was, but Sam didn't deserve — "

Kix couldn't finish his sentence. Suddenly there was a lump in his throat that stopped him.

He took a deep breath. "They say you did it because — "

Again he didn't finish his sentence. *Because you went loony*, that was what he wanted to say. *Loony . . . we don't call people that*, Mom said. Mom, who was still asleep and had no idea what was happening.

"Go on, say it," growled Flint. "Because I went crazy. Stark raving mad. I lost it. Everyone says so, and it's true."

He took a step forward.

Kix jumped, and so did Sam, who half-turned away.

Flint stayed where he was. He pointed at Kix. He pointed with his cigarette hand. The red dot was now signaling from very close by.

"What do you expect?" he snarled. "So your whole farm and all the work you've put into it goes bust, eh? And they show up at your door with papers you don't even understand, and you just want to be outside with your animals, and everything you've built up comes crashing down — what do you think you'd do, you stupid toddler in slippers? Eh?"

Kix felt like crying. He felt like crying very badly. But the tears didn't come.

"I don't know," Kix said. "But what did Sam do to . . ."

"SAM? WHO'S SAM? HIS NAME IS NOT SAM!" Flint screamed and Kix looked back at the rifle. Maybe he should run away, maybe Flint was going to start shooting after all. But Flint took a breath and went on talking, and now he sounded normal again. "Don't look at me like that," he said. "I'm not going to shoot anyone, I told you that. Not any people. I'm not . . ."

He started to laugh. "Ha-ha-ha . . . I was going to say,

84

I'm not crazy . . . when I've just been allowed out for my first weekend, and tomorrow they expect me back at the hospital. Ha-ha-ha, back in the nuthouse . . ."

Kix couldn't run away. He understood that now. Running away was dangerous. Because he'd heard what he'd heard. *I'm not going to shoot anyone, not any people.*

"Sam . . ." Flint muttered. "Maybe that's not such a bad name. He's got papers, an official pedigree, and that says Nanook. But I always called him Dog. Just Dog. He answered to that too. He's a faithful dog. A good dog. I never had to tell him anything. He always understood everything. A stubborn dog too, actually. Still . . . I have to start over again."

Kix only half understood what Flint was saying. But he'd heard one sentence loud and clear. *I'm not going to shoot anyone, not any people.*

Talking, that was what he needed to do. Keep him talking. As long as Flint was talking, he couldn't use his gun. So Kix asked, "Start over?"

"Yeah, kid. If life doesn't give you a second chance, you have to make one yourself. But what would you know about that? And why am I talking to you anyway? What are you doing here? Go back home, get back into bed, put on some dry pants."

"What do you mean, start over again?"

"You don't know what you're asking, kid."

"Start a new farm?"

"Ha!"

Flint threw another cigarette butt into the grass. Kix saw it glow and then go out. *Talk,* he thought, *keep talking.*

"You could, couldn't you?" Kix asked.

"Ha!" Flint said again. "I'm thinking more of ending it. Money gone, stock gone. Destroying everything, moving. Wiping the slate clean and then, one day, maybe . . ."

He turned away and didn't finish his sentence.

Then he looked back at Kix. Softly, very softly, he said, "I don't want to dream, eh? You understand? It was dreams that made everything go wrong. Now I want to be hard. Put it all behind me. Wipe the slate clean. That's why I was out here tonight. That's why I wanted to have Nanook here. Sam. To leave it all behind, dig a hole and then . . ."

Now Kix understood perfectly. He'd understood before too, but now he knew for sure, more than sure. His whole head started to tingle, pins in his brain and in his hair. He looked at Sam. He wanted to grab Sam and hug him, he wanted to protect him, he wanted to stand in front of Sam with his whole body, because what Flint had said about leaving it all behind, digging a hole and then . . . that could only mean he wanted to shoot Sam.

Dead.

Wipe the slate clean.

31

Sam had even wagged his tail when he first saw Flint. Sam recognized his master. Sam had forgotten that Flint had kicked him. Sam was too scared to go near people who were standing up straight, but he didn't remember *why* he was too scared to go near people who were standing up straight. *Sam still loved Flint.*

And Flint had a gun. With bullets in it. One shot in the night. The hole was already dug. Flint had said so.

Kix's head was full of pinpricks and he said, "N-no. No, Mr. Flint, please don't. Sam's already forgotten about the sheep. Sam has new sheep now. I mean us. And he's got Jill and Study and Patriot, and they're his new horses. Sam came to us himself, because he doesn't want to wipe the slate clean. He's already brave enough to be petted again, sometimes all day long, and he plays with Springer, and he's got a new life. Really. He isn't even Nanook anymore. A dog can't hold onto all those things in its brain, Mr. Flint, he's got new things in his brain. He wants to be kind to everyone. Well, not intruders, of course, because he's a watchdog, but now he's with us, he chose us himself and . . . and . . ."

. . . *And he doesn't want to die.* That was what Kix wanted to say. During all this talk he'd moved closer to Flint. He didn't understand how he could be so brave, but he was.

And Flint was listening.

Flint's expression wasn't strange anymore. It was friendlier. Something about his face was changing. He was listening to what Kix was telling him, and for a moment Kix thought it was going to work. He'd say, *Sam doesn't want to die*, and Flint would agree with him.

But Kix didn't get a chance to say it.

Because suddenly someone else was there with them on the grass.

Kix turned to look, and Flint turned to look.

It was Dad.

And Dad had a gun too.

32

Dad held his rifle tight. He hurried over to Kix and — without taking his eyes off Flint for a moment — wrapped an arm around him and shoved him half behind him, as if he wanted Kix to hide behind him, as if Kix was five, no older than Emilia. *Dad*, Kix wanted to say, *Dad, what are you doing?* But he didn't say it, because that would have been childish. And he'd almost done it! He'd seen it in Flint's face. Flint had almost understood him! Kix had come very close to being allowed to take Sam home with him.

Now Flint looked like he'd looked at first. Dark. Confusing.

Kix hadn't even known that Dad had a gun. But here Dad stood, holding his gun tight.

Flint had swung his rifle around to the front too.

He looked at Dad and smiled his Loony-Flint smile. "Ah, the neighbor, I presume."

"Let my son go," Dad said. "Let him go."

"Ha!" said Flint, and Kix said, "Dad . . ." Because Dad didn't understand what had been happening.

Flint was still laughing. "So, neighbor," he said, "how about a smoke?"

He searched for another cigarette.

Kix came up alongside Dad. "Dad . . ." he began again, but Dad pushed him back behind him again.

All this time Sam had been watching from a distance. He'd half-turned away so he could run off if he needed to. He listened and watched, but stood there as if he'd just happened to walk past. Maybe he looked a little nervous, but it could just as easily have been curiosity about what would happen next.

"We're not smoking anything!" Dad exclaimed. He still sounded angry, and that wasn't very smart. *Don't, Dad,* thought Kix, *I had already almost . . .*

"Cool it, man," said Flint. "Relax . . . the boy's here for the dog."

Yeah, thought Kix, *it's all about Sam!*

But Dad didn't relax. He was breathing fast and loud. He reached behind for Kix and — *Huh?* — Kix felt Dad's hand shaking.

And when Dad started talking again, his voice was suddenly twice as loud and twice as angry. "I'LL JUST SAY THIS ONE MORE TIME," Dad shouted, "let my boy go! I'll pay, alright! Six hundred, you said? I'll bring a check in the morning! Six hundred for the dog. If you like, I'll make it cash!"

But then things really started going wrong. Loony-Flint hurled away the cigarette he'd just taken out, without even lighting it. He threw away the lighter as well and gripped his gun with both hands. As if he was going to start shooting any minute now, that's how he held it.

"MONEY?" he screamed. "THIS IS ABOUT MONEY? DO YOU THINK THAT'S WHY I'M STANDING HERE WITH THIS KID OF YOURS WHO WET HIS PANTS EVEN THOUGH I'D NEVER HURT A LITTLE KID?!"

He slid the strap of his rifle off his shoulder and kept

91

the barrel pointing at the ground. The ground between him and Dad.

Sam didn't like shouting. He backed up, disappearing into the greenish-black darkness.

"Flint . . ." Dad said. And he gripped his gun with two hands again as well. As if he might start shooting any minute now too.

"YOU'RE A JERK, YOU KNOW THAT?" Flint screamed. "I wanted to start over again, here! Wipe the slate clean! I was just standing here listening to your little kid and then you show up with your six hundred dollars. Who do you take me for? One of those pigs from the bank? Someone you can buy off? That's not what this is about, you moron! SIX HUNDRED FILTHY DOLLARS!"

"Dad!" Kix shouted. "Dad!"

He was so scared — scared that everyone would

start shooting and then there'd be blood everywhere, everywhere!

But then in the middle of all the shouting they heard another voice. "Sam!" they heard. "Sam! Sam! Sam! Sam!" It was a tiny little voice and high and teary. "Sam! Sam!" It was Emilia. With Mom running after her and shouting, "Emilia!" and then, "Kix! Emilia! Jason! Kix!"

Kix didn't understand. What was his sister doing here? And Mom? And Flint didn't know which way to turn either. Because there was also a lightning-fast dark-brown dog flying along with all these new people. Springer tore around in circles between and past everyone. She was looking for Sam, Sam in the greenish-black darkness, and suddenly she'd found him and was thrumming along in a

straight line toward him. Oh, and look, there — panting and old — there was Holly!

Flint raised his rifle and looked from left to right. There was a wild look in his eyes.

"I couldn't stop her!" Mom said, and Kix didn't know if she meant Emilia or Springer or maybe even Holly.

But now Mom saw Flint's rifle. She immediately grabbed Emilia and pulled her back, into her arms.

"Sam . . ." Emilia said, but now Emilia saw the two guns and the two men too.

Dad had raised his gun up as high as Flint's. The two rifles pointed at each other. That wasn't good. That wasn't good at all.

"Flint . . ." Dad said. "Flint . . ."

They stood facing each other, and everyone and everything went quiet. Only Sam and Springer and Holly were making sounds. Playing sounds.

Flint stared furiously at all the people around him.

Suddenly a door opened behind him. "Flint?" someone said.

Flint screamed, "Dad, stay there!"

"Flint!" Mr. Jones called out again. "I heard everything. That six hundred dollars was my idea. I suggested that! Don't do anything crazy, son!"

"CRAAAAAZY!" Flint roared.

Things were going wrong.

"CRAAAAAZY!"

Kix saw it happening. He could feel it everywhere, in his stomach and in his feet, in his head and in the night, it was all going wrong. Flint was turning into Loony-Flint. It was up to Kix to do something. To say something that would turn back time to a few minutes ago. Before Flint's face turned hard again. When Kix had understood what Flint meant. That was why he took a breath. That was why he took a step to the side, coming out from behind Dad's back. And that was why he shouted, "Sam's the boss! Dad! Flint! STOP IT! SAM'S THE BOSS!"

33

"Kix . . ." Dad started, but Flint was looking at Kix now. His eyes looked wild and weird.

"What!" he said.

It didn't sound like a question, but it was.

Kix took another deep breath. His throat felt raw and painful, maybe because that lump was back again or maybe because his heart had leapt up into it. Kix said, "Sam is the boss. That's what Mom said. So Sam has to decide. He can, too. He knows what he wants, so you have to put the guns away and then we'll let Sam decide."

Flint blinked.

Kix took two more steps to the side and then two forward.

"Kix!" Dad said, and Mom screamed it out too: "KIX!"

But Kix did what he had to do. And he said it again, "Flint, Dad, let's let Sam decide. He can do it. He knows what he wants. Sam's the boss."

Kix said it because suddenly he knew that it was true. It wasn't up to the people. Sam had to decide. That was scary and terrible, because Sam might choose Flint. He'd had a reason for wagging his tail just now, Kix hadn't forgotten that. And if Sam chose Flint, Kix would be so sad it would make him sick. He'd stay in bed for months and months, and so would Emilia. They'd cry until they didn't have any tears left to cry. Their stomachs would hurt and their hearts would want to stop beating, but they'd still know that it had to be that way. This wasn't up to the people. Kix was sure of that, and he knew that Emilia was sure of it too. If they had to give up Sam, they would. But not because grown-ups were fighting over him. Not because grown-ups had guns in their hands. If they had to give up Sam, it would be because Sam had chosen to go back to his old life. To his old master. To Flint.

And so Kix stepped up to the thrown-away lighter. He picked it up, along with the cigarette.

He walked over to Flint and held out his hands. Just like he had to do with Sam when he wanted to pet him. He held out his hands, open, with the cigarette and lighter. He stopped and waited. Just like he had to do with Sam.

Flint stared at Kix's hands.

Dad lowered his rifle. Kix saw that out of the corner of his eye.

And then Flint did the same thing. He lowered his rifle. He lifted the strap back up and hooked it over his shoulder. Then he swung the gun around to his side.

Nobody said anything.

Kix was still standing there with outstretched arms and open hands.

No, nobody said anything. Not Dad, not Mom, not Emilia, and not Mr. Jones. The dogs were still playing further off in the darkness.

It took forever and ever, but finally Flint looked Kix in the eye.

He reached out and took the lighter first and then the cigarette.

Kix lowered his arms.

He hugged himself tight, because it was cold.

But he stayed standing there.

Flint put the cigarette in his mouth. He cupped his hands and flicked up the lid of the lighter. He held his head a little to one side, and in the light of the flame behind Flint's fingers, Kix caught another glimpse of the face he had seen earlier.

This wasn't the face of a Loony-Flint. This was the face of someone who had lost his sheep and horses and was trying to figure out how to start over again.

And that meant he'd say yes. Kix was sure of it.

Yes, Sam would have to choose.

Sam had almost his whole new flock around him now — Kix, Emilia, Mom, Dad, Holly, Springer. Only the horses were missing.

But Flint was there too. His master. His sheep farmer master.

It was scary and terrible, but Sam would have to choose. And Sam could do it. Everyone was there.

Flint would say yes. Kix was cold to his bones, but it was the only way. It was the only way.

Flint blew out another stream of smoke, a stream that turned into a cloud.

He coughed.

He wiped something away from his mouth.

He looked at Kix and said, "No."

34

Flint said no.

Kix's shoulders sagged. The night breeze hit his pajama bottoms, the wet spot. Maybe he should turn away, maybe he should let them shoot each other, maybe everything was over now.

He had thought he understood Flint. He had thought Flint had understood him. But he really was just a little kid. Maybe he'd just been dreaming again. Fairy-tale ghost nonsense.

"No," Flint said again. "No, we're not doing that. The dog doesn't have to choose. The dog already chose."

What? Kix looked up. He tried to make out Flint's expression. *What did he mean?*

Flint now turned directly toward Kix. "I'm his master. I *was* his master. And a good master doesn't leave the decisions to his sheepdog."

Kix almost understood. But not entirely.

"No," Flint said. The crack in his voice seemed to have grown even bigger. "As far as I'm concerned, all a sheepdog has to do is watch over its flock. You were right, kid. Before. And now too. You're his flock. All of you. So take him."

Then Flint turned around. He started walking toward his father. Toward the house.

Kix was still standing there. Dad, too, and Mom and Emilia. They were all standing there. They didn't move because they weren't sure if they understood what had happened.

Flint turned around one last time, looking at Kix again. "What are you doing there?" he shouted. "I already told you, the dog's made its choice. So get out of here. And put on some clean clothes while you're at it. You're starting to stink."

35

It was only when they got home that Kix started to shake. He couldn't stop either.

Flint had turned his back on them again and walked past Mr. Jones and into the house. Mom had run over to Kix. She'd knelt in front of him and thrown her arms around him. Dad followed Flint, and Emilia called Sam. "Sam!" she shouted. "Springer! Holly! Springer! Holly! Sam! We're going home."

They'd come to her, all three of them. As if they belonged together: one dog for Mom, one dog for Dad, one dog for Kix and Emilia.

And that was right — they did belong together now. Kix was sure of it. He saw it when Sam turned and walked toward them. Springer skipped along behind Dad, who maybe still wanted to talk to Mr. Jones. Holly stumbled over to Emilia. But Sam walked to Kix.

No, he walked past Kix. On his way home. But he made sure to brush past Kix's hand. And when he did, Kix felt the soft hair between his fingers. Snowy hair, but warm. Fairy-tale hair, but real. And when Kix felt that, and when he was sure that Sam was going to be staying with them now, that was when he got freezing cold. He stiffened up completely. His body refused to move another inch. Mom had to lift him up as if he was five, or four, younger even than Emilia.

"Mom," Kix cried in her ear, "Sam almost got — "

He didn't finish his sentence, because Mom said soothing words and soothing phrases, and she also said that she'd be proud of him forever. Kix only half heard, because the sentence he'd been going to say was still pounding in his head. SAM. ALMOST. GOT. KILLED.

It was as if he only then realized it. They crossed their own yard on the gravel drive. Sam crawled under the fence to the field. Maybe he wanted to tell Jill and Study and Patriot what had happened. "Let him go," Mom said, "that's his spot. That's where he wants to be now."

And then they went into the house and the light. But the moment they were inside, Kix started trembling and shivering all over. His teeth chattered, his hands shook, and it was a good thing that Mom was still carrying him in

her arms, otherwise he would have collapsed in a heap on the floor: his knees had stopped working too.

Emilia stared at him with big eyes. Maybe she thought the shaking was scary. Maybe she thought he'd gone crazy.

36

Mom made some hot chocolate and ran a bath so Kix could get clean and warm up again.

After he'd been in the water for a while, he stopped trembling. Now he was just tired.

But he still didn't want to go to bed.

He didn't have to either, because Dad came back from across the road. He went into the bathroom, knelt down next to the bath, and hugged Kix tight.

While Kix was pressed up against Dad's chest — making his shirt wet, but that didn't matter — he heard what Dad said: "Son, oh, son . . . I'll never do anything like that again, I promise. Your sister woke up and found out you weren't in your bed. She woke us up and told us where you must have gone. I ran straight there like an idiot. I almost ruined everything. But you, son, you understood it all and saved the day . . ."

"Dat . . ." Kix mumbled against Dad's chest. His mouth was a bit squashed and the words came out funny, "Dat, I dint eefen know you hat a huntin ghun . . ."

"Oh, son," Dad said, squeezing even harder.

"DAT!" Kix said.

"Oh, sorry," said Dad. "I'm squeezing the life out of you."

He let go, and Kix said, "That's alright, but can I have some more hot water?"

"Of course," Dad said. He turned on the tap, and Kix felt the wonderful hot water flowing near his feet.

"You're going to bed soon, eh?" Dad said, standing up. Kix nodded. "Good. Mom will be in in a sec." But at the door, Dad turned back for a moment. "Kixie," he said, "are you still angry?"

Kix looked at Dad's wet knees. *Angry?* he thought. *Was I angry? Oh, yeah, earlier in the night, when I screamed into my pillow.* He could hardly remember it. "That's too long ago," he said. "I've already forgotten it."

Dad laughed and then, through the bathroom wall, they heard Mom taking Emilia to bed. Emilia was begging for a bedtime story.

"I want one too," Kix said. "About the pig that loves hot buttered toast. It's funny, and Mom wanted to read it tomorrow, but it's almost tomorrow now."

Dad laughed again. He was still standing at the door. "I'll pass that along," he said.

"Okay," said Kix.

He wasn't cold anymore. He had just one more question. It was about Flint. "Will it turn out alright?" Kix asked.

And it was great because now Dad understood. Dad understood him perfectly and right away! "I'll go see him tomorrow," he said. "I promise. Flint has to go back to the hospital, but before he does, I'll go talk to him. It might take a while, but in the end I'm sure it will all work out. Yes. I'm sure of it."

Great. Kix nodded.

He said, "Will you ask Mom? *Captain Underpants* is okay too. Two chapters. No, three."

37

A little later Kix was lying in bed listening to Mom's voice. Two sentences. Three. But he was so sleepy, he couldn't really manage it.

Soon he was sound asleep, and he slept for a long time.

Only once did he wake up. For just a moment. It was still nighttime.

Kix peered into the darkness around him. The stars were glowing on the ceiling. His slippers were next to the bed. And the books he loved were on the nightstand.

But was that a train Kix heard? He wasn't sure. Maybe he was still dreaming.

It was howling, of course. The howl of a dog.

Sam, Kix thought happily. *That's our Sam. Flint was right.* And he'd been right too. Sam had made his choice. For him. For here.

But Kix had been wrong too. Sam wasn't a sad dog. Sam had made a new start long ago. With a clean slate. Did that howl sound sad? Did it sound like Sam was echoing the trains?

No. If you listened closely, maybe it wasn't even howling. If you listened closely, it was — he was almost sure of it . . . if you listened closely, Kix thought, it was like cheering.

That's right. Sam was cheering. *Wow, wow-wow-wow!*

It made Kix laugh. *Wow, wow-wow-wow!*

He was sure he'd hear it lots more. Sam's cheering. Sam's long and happy *Wow!*

A Note from the Author

This book is not a made-up story.

In the summer of 2010, I was on vacation at my brother's farm in Canada. In a part of the country that is still visited by wolves and coyotes. A snow-white dog showed up and stayed with us. He had chosen us as his flock. We called him Sam, even though he was already called Nanook.

Gradually we found out what had happened to him. This story is based on all the things we heard and all the things that happened afterwards.

That's why I would like to especially thank René van de Vendel and Karen Christie, my brother and his wife. And their children: Nicolette, Anthony, Matthew, and Anna. The grandmas and grandpas too: Dick and Rieta van de Vendel and Jamie and Marilynn Christie. Oh, and of course, the horses and dogs: Sal, Bailey, Trail, Keysha, and Ruka. And Captain the cat, who didn't even make it into this book.

But, above all, thanks to Sam. He's the fairy-tale dog that really exists.

Edward

P.S. The books Kix reads are about the little pig Mercy Watson (written by Kate DiCamillo and illustrated by Chris Van

Dusen) and about the adventures of Captain Underpants (written and illustrated by Dav Pilkey).

P.P.S. Flint is doing well.